Addicted to You

by

Ja'Kwontez Glover

RoseDog Books
PITTSBURGH, PENNSYLVANIA 15238

RoseDog Books
585 Alpha Drive, Suite 103
Pittsburgh, PA 15238
Visit our website at *www.rosedogbookstore.com*

ISBN: 979-8-89127-560-7
eISBN: 979-8-89127-058-9

Love, Sex, and Handcuffs

"Maybe it's best that I set myself free. Is it possible that I liked you more than the person I am? Or maybe it's only the sadness of a lover," I said to myself.

As I sat in despair, I could hear my coworker say, "Beware. They may have game…but their tongues speak with lies, pleading to kind hearts for a prize." I was head over heels with both of these guys. I was in too deep. I've got nothing left. I have no life. I'm dead inside. I'm sorry. I'm finished. I've sold my soul to both. Crying. Holding a gun to my head. Wanting to end it all. Tears flooded my eyes. Hello. My name is Jasmine. Jasmine McKenna. And this is my story of how I fell in love with another guy and destroyed my marriage.

Before all this happened, I was married. Five years, to be exact. To my wonderful husband, Marcus McKenna. Now Marcus is very professional and successful. Everywhere he went he got treated as a celebrity. The spotlight was always on him. Yes. It bothered me how much attention he would get when out in public. He would always tell me, "Baby, I don't want them other females. You are the only one for me." "I trust you," I'd say, but in the back of my mind I knew I couldn't trust him. I would hear voices in my head saying, *He's a liar.* I got to be honest. I had trust issues. When you give someone everything and they treat it like nothing, something inside of you really breaks. I was that girl who was a little clingy. I will accept it. I am because of people who have left before. I don't want to lose anyone else. So I hold on for dear life to make sure they are happy. But it comes off as me being needy. I am not just scared. If I cling to you, I am afraid to lose you. I feel like you leave. I will cling to you but won't trust you. Because of things others have done. Lying. Pretending to be my friend. When instead they are just around to ruin my reputation. To make my life terrible. To beat me down lower than I already was. So I am sorry for being clingy. For not trusting. But I can't help it. Because others hurt me so badly that my heart is so broken. It is impossible to back the pieces. It got so bad that I had to go to therapy. My therapist also used to tell me that I needed to give myself some space and make time for myself. I took the therapy advice. You see, I knew my husband was an important man. His phone used to ring back to back and he would leave, going on business trips that would keep us apart nearly three months at a time whenever we tried to spend time with each other. Yeah. I got upset. But I knew what I was getting myself into. At that moment I grew lonely, due to the fact my husband was away on a business trip.

As I grew lonely I began to write in my journal:

"Beauty, the world seemed to say. And as if to prove it

(scientifically) wherever he looked at the houses, at the railings, at the antelopes stretching over the palings, beauty sprang instantly. To watch a leaf quivering in the rush of air was an exquisite joy. Up in the sky swallows swooping, swerving, flinging themselves in and out, 'round and 'round, yet always with perfect control as if elastics held them; and the flies rising and falling; and the sun spotting now this leaf, now that, in mockery, dazzling it with soft gold in pure good temper; and now again some chime (it might be a motor horn) tinkling divinely on the grass stalks—all of this, calm and reasonable as it was, made out of ordinary things as it was, was the truth now; beauty, that was the truth now. Beauty was everywhere."

Before I could finish I began to cry. I went to sleep closing my eyes, beginning to dream of broken butterflies tearing lovely monarch wings on faithless love that angels sing...I find shiny metal in the kitchen sink in an evening absent light. I find peace in cuts of pink, watching crimson blood flow feels so right. Starlight shines upon my tears. The voices began to speak to me. "You cannot bleed all of your suicidal fears at night when you begin to cry. I'll sing you a lover's lullaby." My love, do not wish that you were dead dreaming of an absent pulse lying on silken sheets bleeding red. I will offer love so do not bleed, give me your knife, I am all you need.... At that moment I was hopeless. One of my friends was concerned so she introduced me to this online dating site called *Match.com*. I'm old-fashioned. I didn't know much about the site. My friend explained everything to me. At first I was scared, I didn't want to do anything that would hurt my marriage.

"I don't know. I don't think I should be on something like this. What if my husband finds out about this? How would he be when he is on the move?"

"Just try it and if you don't like it, you can delete it."

"Okay, I trust you," I said.

"You will be fine."

I spent hours on that dating site. I became overwhelmed due to all the requests and responses I was getting. I didn't want to talk to anyone. I was afraid to pursue an online relationship. My anxiety began to attack me. I started to panic, worry, darkness closing in around me.

These are some of the words I could use to describe my anxiety, but nothing I can say could speak of its entirety as I cry internally, thinking I've lost my sanity. Every time I go to the doctor's, counselor's, they say there's something wrong with me. My friends tell me to calm down and stop being so crazy. But how can I calm down when the world around me is spinning out of control and I can barely see? Then suddenly. A soft voice whispered to me.

"Breathe. You will get through this."

I know I be overreacting about the silliest little things, but to me those silly little things seem like the doom the world could bring. Can't you see, a spilled glass of milk to you can seem like an earthquake to me. Once again that soft voice whispered to me.

"Breathe. You will get through this."

Suddenly, I closed my eyes and took a deep breath. All my worries and stress left as if it didn't exist. I felt like a new person. As I began my search for a companion, this particular profile by the name of Michael Jones who kept liking my pictures, leaving sweet romantic quotes on my page. Even sending me messages in my inbox. He pursued me as if I was some type of celebrity or something. I let him chase some more, then I got tired of the chase so I decided to write to him.

Jasmine: Hey.

Johnathan: Hey, I'm surprised that you wrote me back. I'm sorry if I came off as a creep by liking your pictures and flooding your inbox.

Jasmine: Oh, no, you okay. I'm wondering, why me? What makes me so interesting?

Johnathan: It's your presence. I kinda felt as if you needed someone to talk to.

Jasmine: Yeah, I feel lonely due to my husband taking business trips and leaving me all alone three months at a time.

Johnathan: Oh, I didn't know you were married,

how long you been married and do you have any kids?

Jasmine: Yeah, we've been married for almost five years and no, we don't have any kids due to his work schedule. Is that a problem?

Johnathan: No, not at all. Oh, I'm sorry, where's my manners? I'm Johnathan. Johnathan Banks.

Jasmine: It's okay, I'm Jasmine. Jasmine McKenna.

Johnathan: Wow, that's a unique name, I like. Is it okay if we get to know each other?

Jasmine: Thank you, my grandmother named me and yes, it's okay if we can get to know each other. Well, I'm about to log off, I got to get dinner ready, I talk to you later.

Johnathan: Before you log out, can we exchange numbers?

Jasmine: Sure, what's your number?

Johnathan: (375) 349-2267.

Jasmine: Okay, I'll talk to you soon.

Johnathan: Okay.

See. Right then I shouldn't write him back due to me being married. Because all of the attention he was giving me, it made me feel wanted. Every day and night I would receive sweet romantic poems and songs that were requested by him. The way he carried on made me fall deeply in love with me. I haven't felt that way in a long time. This gentleman knew how to make a woman feel special. I was head over heels for him. I even took a chance of him coming over to my house. The third night we had sex.

He whispered in my ear, "I crave your mouth, your voice, your hair."

Silent and starving, I prowled through the streets. Bread does not nourish me, dawn disrupts me, all day I hunt for the liquid measure of your steps. Then he started tonguing my ear. Blushing. I was turned on. I love the way he fucked me. I should have quit while I had a chance. I still would have been married until this day but noooo, my curiosity got the best of me. I couldn't help it. The moment felt so right. I waited almost three days getting back online. I felt ashamed. I was in love with my online lover. I didn't know how to tell my husband, so I had a conversation with my friend about the situation. She was totally in shock.

"How are you going to tell your husband?"

"To be honest I really don't know."

I was confused. Three months later my husband made it home from his business trip. We were both happy to see each other.

"How was your trip?"

"It was good, I've landed a lot of business deals but I'm more happy to see you."

"Me too," as a grin formed on my face.

"What's for dinner?"

"I've ordered takeout."

"Takeout?"

"Yeah. It's this new restaurant that just opened up."

"What restaur—"

Before he could say anything else, I pressed my lips against his and led him to the bathroom, where rose petals awaited him. We began to make love.

"Your eyes, your lips, your hands, I miss, your kiss, your touch, that fire so much. I'm under your spell, I'm so hot for you, my soul burns in hell. My toes curl, as you play with my hair, my tummy tingles, every time you are near. Heat, blazing, intense, like a furnace I go up in flames. With you by my side, around me, inside me, I soar to the sky, you're with me, you guide me. Your lips on my skin, your fingers within, your breath on my neck, your legs within mine, you're glistening; sweat, you're feeling my fire. Take me higher again, I wanna go to heaven!"

Less than three hours, we were done. He rolled over and kissed my forehead as I sucked my thumb. I was in my happy moment. Six minutes later I was woken to a ring at the door. Wondering who that would be, rushing out of bed carefully not to awaken my king, covering my naked body. As I made it to the living room, I peeked out the window. Oh. It was the dinner I ordered.

"Babe, food here!" as I yelled from the living room.

As I was preparing dinner, my phone instantly

started going off. Looking at my phone, I noticed it was my secret online lover, Johnathan. Why was he sending me messages knowing my husband was back from his business trip?

"What are you doing?" I said in fear. "My husband's home, I can't talk to you right now."

"But my love, I missed you, you haven't responded to any of my messages."

"Now is not the time, my husband is home."

He started to get aggravated due to the fact I didn't want to communicate with him. I instantly blocked him. I realized that was a bad idea. I later regretted blocking him, but little did I know he was going to destroy my marriage in the long run.

As I was getting dinner prepared, my husband saw despair on my face. "What's wrong?"

"Nothing, everything fine. Are you ready to eat, hun?"

God, why did I just lie to my husband? I hoped this didn't haunt me.

"You know you can talk to me."

"Everything fine," as I kissed his lips.

"Okay, I'm here for you."

"Yes. I know. Now are you hungry, hun?"

"Sure. What did you order?"

"I've ordered your favorite, French Dip Sandwich."

"Sounds good. Hun, you know how to find a way to my heart," as he kissed my forehead.

I couldn't do anything but blush.

After dinner I joined him in the shower. As the cool water streamed down upon my hot, sweaty body, leaning my head back, the water fell upon my face. He caressed the roundness of my full breasts with his thumb and forefinger squeezing my nipples. A moan escaped from my sensual lips. Slowly his hands moved down to caress my stomach. A surge of electricity ran through my body. Though I was in cool water, my body was on fire. Closing my eyes, my mind wandered, thinking of my lover, his hand moving to my inner thighs. Slowly he moved it up to my womanhood. My breathing became more rapid, body tense. As his fingers began to lightly rub me, I dreamed that he was kneeling between my legs. His strong fingertips were touching my budding nubbin. My body was enraptured by the dream. He finally stood and began kissing me. His hands rubbed all over my dripping-wet breasts. His hands encompassed my silky butt cheeks, surrendering to the thought of excitement.

Driving his fingers deeply between my soft lips, the memory of our lovemaking drove me to heights. His fingers rubbed and caressed quicker as I gasped hard. The electricity filled my loins and in flames my senses screamed as the orgasm overwhelmed me. He then proceeded to lift me up from the shower and placed me onto the bed, eating my pussy. I pushed his head forward as his tongue went deeper and deeper. As my pussy began to gush out cum, looking up at me his sexy eyes met mine as I bit my lips.

"Best sex ever," I said as I fell dead to the world.

Three hours later I was woken to text messages.

Johnathan: Hey, baby, I miss you.

Johnathan: Why you not responding to my call?

Johnathan: Baby, I love you, please respond back.

Johnathan: 😘

I responded....

Jasmine: Who is that?

Johnathan: Baby, stop playing games, this is your secret lover. Johnathan. Remember?

Jasmine: How are you still texting me when I blocked your number?

Johnathan: Baby, you can't get rid of me that easy, besides I've changed my number just to talk to you.

Jasmine: What do you want?

Johnathan: I just wanted to talk to you. I missed you, baby.

Jasmine: Things been okay, I told you my husband back from his business trip and I really can't talk due to him here.

Johnathan: You don't love me anymore.

Jasmine: I do...it just....

Johnathan: Just what?

Jasmine: Nothing. I have to go.

****BLOCKED****

My husband noticed me sitting alone the bed. "What's wrong?" as he placed his hands on my shoulders.

"Nothing, everything is fine. It's just scammers calling me."

"Well, maybe you should block them."

"Yeah, I should."

"Come back to bed," he said as he kissed my forehead.

The next day I woke up to some breakfast in bed and music playing.

"Good morning, my queen," he said as my eyelids lifted, kissing my lips. "I made you some breakfast. Sausages, eggs, grits, French toast, bacon, fruits, coffee, and juice."

"Baby, you're so sweet, that's why I married you."

"You sure not for my money and looks?" he said, laughing.

"No, I married you because you are sweet, respectable, and charming."

That whole day I was treated as a queen. He even took me shopping and got my hair and nails done. Whew. I was overdue for a hairdo. Everything was going well until he got a phone call. I tried to take the phone but he insisted that it was important. I thought I was important. Looking at him in despair.

"Fuck," he said as he got off the phone. "I'm sorry,

bae, but we have to cut today short. I have to fly out to-night. I'm sorry, I promise I will make it up to you."

I pushed him away as he tried to kiss me. "When are you going to make time for me?" I said in rage.

All he could say was "Sorry."

"Fine. Take me home."

As we made it home, I didn't even say two words to him. I stared at him the whole time, rolling my eyes. He made me sick. Perfect day ruined by one phone call.

He left for his flight that night around 9 P.M. I kept forwarding his calls. I was so upset that I unblocked Johnathan's number. *Ring...ring...ring.*

Johnathan: Hello?

Jasmine: Hey, baby, how are you doing? I miss hearing your sexy voice.

Johnathan: Oh, really? Where is your husband?

Jasmine: He left, he had to go out of town.

Johnathan: Oh, okay.

Jasmine: Yeah. I'm bored, I want some company.

Johnathan: Oh, yeah?

Jasmine: Yeah. Come over.

Johnathan: Okay, give me an hour, I'm about to hop into the shower.

Jasmine: Me too.

Two hours later the doorbell rang. It was my online lover. I greeted him with my sexy see-through lingerie gown on, a kiss, and hung.

"Baby, I've missed you."

"I've missed you too. Don't have me waiting like that anymore," he said, smiling.

"I promise I won't," as I pulled him in the house so the neighbors wouldn't be nosy.

"So where did your husband fly out to?"

"Shhhhh, never mind that," as I began to unbutton his pants.

He began to lose words as I pleasured him. I got up from my knees and led him into the bedroom. I began to put on a sex show for him. Lap dance not costing nothing for him except a box of gloves and a bottle of gin to me, that's more than a bargain. As I lay under him, legs wrapped tightly around his waist, a twenty-four-hour love affair getting flirty and dirty, love when he pulled my hair cumming like poetry without a care, rising off the bed. As my pussy began to become wet, his tongue moved in swirls.

"You're so wet and tight," he said in excitement.

His fingers entered deep, stroking my G-spot so sweet till my yoni wept. I began to grip him so tight as he tongue-whipped me just right. I moaned with delight. Lapping every stream wouldn't stop until I screamed, releasing my cream. I started cumming back to back from the tongue of my lover.

"Your nectar is so sweet, even sugar can't compete

every time you skeet," he said, pulling out.

I needed that relief.

As we lay in bed, I could feel his dick push against my ass.

"I see someone excited again."

"Yeah, I am. What are you going to do about it?"

"Don't tempt me," I said, laughing.

"Babe, can I ask you a question?"

"Sure, what's up?"

"How long are we going to keep this affair going?"

"As long as you want."

"I want it to last long at the same time, I want you to leave your husband and be with me."

"Now you know I can't do that."

"Why?"

"I just can't, that's my husband and we've been together for almost six years. I'm sorry."

"Do you love me?"

"I do."

"Okay, that's a good reason."

"I told you I can't."

"Well, I feel that you should let him know before he gets hurt finding out in the long run."

"Sigh. Give me some time. I will tell him when the time is right but not now. Now, give me some more dick."

After going three rounds, we both were dead to

the world.

I was woken to keys jingling in the front door. I jumped up. Marcus.

"Johnathan, get up, my husband here."

"Wha…what's wrong?"

"You got to go."

"Why?"

"My husband is here."

"Shit."

He jumped up naked, trying to find his clothes. I could hear my husband making his way down the hallway. I pushed him in the closet and told him to be quiet.

"Hunni, I'm home."

"Wow, what a surprise, you got home early."

"Yeah. I didn't not go due to having memories of you playing in my mind, saying, 'When am I going to make time for you?' You're right, I do need to make time. Bae, you is the most important thing to me. I mean, we've been married for almost six years. Marriage is important."

At that moment tears began to form in my eyes.

"That's all I wanted, just to spend time with you, wife. Baby, I love you and I love you too. I'm going to treat you to dinner and a shopping spree, but first I have to go jump in the shower."

As he made his way into the shower, I rushed into

the room.

"What the hell is going on? I thought your husband was out of town?"

"I thought so too. I'm sorry but I can't do this anymore."

"I'm sorry, Jasmine. So, are you just going to up and quit?"

"I can't believe you saying this right now. I've opened my life to you and even risked my marriage for you. How could you? Why me?" as tears flow down my face.

"Jasmine, okay, I'm sorry. No, I didn't mean it like that but you need to tell him."

"I will tell him, please give me more time."

"When?" he said as he began to put on his clothes.

"Tonight, I promise."

"Good, 'cause I can't keep doing this walking quietly into the living room. I can't live another moment without you."

"I feel that way about you as well. I'll call you later," after giving him a quick kiss on the lips, closing the door behind him.

I sat on the couch motionless, thinking about the damage I was causing my marriage. How could one conversation and one-night stand cause damage? How would my life be when he found out? Was he going to be cool? What? I don't know. Sigh. How could I be so lost in a place I know so well? How could I be so broken in a marriage so together? How could I be so lonely? Surrounded by so many? How could I be so unhappy? Surrounded by so much beauty? How could I be me? When even I remain a mystery?

As I placed my face in my hands, I didn't notice my husband was in the hallway listening.

"Hunni, are you okay? What's wrong? You can talk to me," as he placed his arms around my hopeless body.

"It's nothing. I just had a flashback on the life I've once had."

"You don't have to worry about that lifestyle any-more. What's done in the past is the past, move on, things happen for reasons. Life lessons are so precious, take them wherever you go. In every experience, no matter the age. Grow wiser and accept what you know. Seems as if we learn something new every day, mistakes arise but they can be fixed. Don't quit, move forward each day. Accepting ups and downs, don't get signals mixed. Life teaches us to be strong, resilient, and keep hope alive. Grow in confidence each day that passes by. No matter how hard life may knock us down each time. We'll stand back up and won't fail to thrive," as he lifted my chin, pressing his lips against mine.

"I love you, Jon...I meant Marcus."

"What?"

"Nothing. That slipped out."

"Who is Jon?"

"I don't know. I didn't mean to say that, I meant you," as I started to hug him. "You know you're the only one for me. I love you, hubby."

"I hear you," as a grin formed on his face.

At that moment we had an argument.

"You know, sometimes I do not know how to stop the things I say. Quickly building a defense against what comes and what may. Confused most of the time about what's going on. Not sure what, why, when, or how these things begin/began. At moment of fight the anger, the hurt takes flight. The feeling that you don't believe in me. That alone I stand and even you I have to make see. That I try so hard and most of the time I'm doing fine. Why carry on and attack me, why aren't certain things just left to be? Only knowing, not wanting to proceed. With these malicious thoughts and evil deeds. I don't want to always feel the need to explain to you my actions, to feel insufficient, to feel mean. I hate the person that lingers inside of me. The one that emerges when the argument arises. The one who looks and seeks disguises. The one who lingers and looks for reasons. The one who seems to always start the fight. I can say sorry in many diff languages and many ways. But you will never see what these little arguments do to me. I can only wonder and hope that you will feel, that you will see. How much I love you and how much to me you mean. I'm done," he said as he walked out, slamming the door behind him.

I fell on my knees, pouring my eyes out. Later that night I tried calling him, but he kept forwarding my calls. As I lay in bed feeling emotionally unavailable, an explosion in my head… *tired of fighting, feeling wrong within, feeling like I am too much, I want to be reached. You see, I want to feel I'm not the only one fighting, don't quit on me. Don't tell me you can't make me happy. Don't tell me it's not exactly what I asked for. Tell me you will do what it takes. You won me before. Win me again.*

At that moment I felt hopeless. I called my online love, Johnathan, "the back-door Jody."

Johnathan: Hello?

Jasmine: Hey, what you doing? (weeping)

Johnathan: Nothing, just getting home, why, what's up?

I began to cry.

Johnathan: Jasmine, what's wrong, why are you crying?

Jasmine: Me and Marcus got into an argument.

Johnathan: Why? What happened?

When I told him the reason behind the argument, Johnathan began to get angry due to me not telling Marcus the truth. He got so angry that he started to curse. I couldn't take the abuse from him, so I just hung up the phone. He made several attempts calling me back. I kept forwarding his calls. I guess he had enough of my nonsense that he decided to come over without my knowledge. As he made it to my house, I heard him knocking. I didn't answer. So he called my phone once more. He was aware of me not answering my phone, so he decided to leave a voice message.

Johnathan: I see you are not answering your phone. I'm wondering why you are playing games. See, that's why I really don't want to deal with you, because you are full of it. How dare you call and cry to me about your situation. You know what, I'm done with you. I hope your husband find out the truth."

I heard him walk off my doorstep. I peeped out the window. I watched him get in his car, slamming the door and driving off as if he was driving in a NASCAR series. I sat and watched my lover disappear into the night.

That night I cried myself to sleep. I found myself waking up to my husband eating my pussy.

Looking up at me, he said, "I'm sorry, I didn't mean to hurt you," and before I could say anything he placed his finger on my lips and began to eat my pussy.

I positioned myself in the "69" position and started sucking his dick. I was in the mood at that point. I began to say sexual things to him. "Fuck me, my pussy is wet, I want to feel you. I want you to take my body and make it your own. I'm throbbing, my pussy wants to feel your dick. I want you to make me cum as I dig into the bed with my nails as you taste me."

We made love for two hours. He fucked so good that I just lay in his arms as his heart beat against head as it rested upon his chest.

As I looked up at my king, he smiled and kissed my forehead, saying, "I will never leave you. Marriage has its ups and downs. I'm willing to do anything that will keep it alive."

At that moment I felt what he said. Man, I loved my husband. Imagining the perfect life that I had. I had a perfect life. It wasn't much but it was enough for me. It kept me alive and happy in a vague way: no dis-appointments on the near horizon, no pangs of doubt; looking forward in anticipation, looking back in satis-faction at the conclusion of each day. I heeded the promptings of my inner voice and what I heard is com-forting, full of reassurance for my own powers and innate superiority—the fake security of someone in the grip of a delusion, in denial, climbing ever-taller towers like a tiny tyrant looking on his little kingdom with a secret smile, while all the while time he lies in wait and what feels ample now turns colorless and cold, and what seems beautiful and strong becomes an object of indifference reaching out to no one, as later middle age turns old, and the strength is gone. Right now the moments yielded to me sweet feelings of contentment, but the human dies, and what I take for granted bears a name to be forgotten soon, as the things I know turn into unfamiliar faces in a strange room, leaving merely a blank space, like a hole left in the wake of a perfect life, which closes over. Sigh.

I was dozing off, sucking my thumb. Last night was a perfect night. No interruptions. Just cuddling and Netflix with the hubby as the breeze outside blew soft and soothing as a caress. Releasing all the stress. The moon began to glow as his brown eyes glowed with the light of the moon. Looking up at him, a smile flowed on his lips like a river. I could hear the leaves fall, listening to their soft rustle. Building a dream castle. As clouds covered the moon, wrapping in deathly silence, I began to relax my body. A hug came and shielded me, giving me all the warmth I needed. In the arms of my hubby, I peacefully fell asleep once again.

I was awakened to my king guiding me into the bedroom in his arms. As he placed me onto the bed, he proceeded with a kiss on my lips, leaving with a "Goodnight, I love you, I will be in soon."

"Okay, don't be long," as I rolled over.

Suddenly my phone began to ring in the distance. Looking for it, I noticed I'd left it in the living room.

"Shit," I said as I jumped up from the bed.

After the fifth ring, my husband answered the phone. I began to bite my nails. Things became silent, then he walked into the room, handing me the phone. I started to have fear.

"When I have fears that I may cease to be," I nervously answered, thinking Johnathan was on the other line. My thoughts began to race.

Jasmine: Hhhhello?

Ashley: Hey, bestie, are you okay?

Jasmine: Oh, yeah, I'm fine.

I was relieved it was my best friend Ashley. My high school friend. If it was Johnathan, I wouldn't know what I would have done.

Ashley: Umm, okay, I was calling to see if we was still on for having a girls' night out this coming Friday.

Jasmine: Girl, you know I'm game. I have to go shopping for something. Girl, you kinda had me scared, I thought it was Johnathan.

Ashley: I'm sorry, I didn't mean to scare you. Girl, what are you going to do about him? What if Marcus answers your phone one day as he calls you?

Jasmine: I don't know what I'm going to do, but I will figure out something, trust me.

Ashley: Okay, girl, just be careful. Well, let me know when you want to hit the shopping mall.

Jasmine: Okay, girl, I see soon, I love you.

Ashley: I love you too, bye.

Jasmine: Bye.

"Damn. That was a close call," I said, holding my heart. Maybe I should put my phone on airplane mode while he was here.

As I lay in bed wondering how my life was spinning out of control, I began to feel pressured. Should I tell him? Should I tell him not? I asked myself as I buried my face into the pillow as I cried. Due to things I'd caused in my marriage, I pretended that I felt fine as I covered a smile in despair. Sadness is easily hidden. I do it so well that no one is aware. Sometimes I go off into a quiet place when I am feeling low. There I shall cry for hours, no one would ever know. It's easy masking sorrow if I keep it out of sight, weeping tears in silence as I hug my pillow tight. Only my pillow will know the tears I cried.

Heartache is never heard when hidden from view. Those tears on my pillow shall be shed silently, yearning goes unnoticed; it hurts, you cannot see.

My husband heard my cries. He lay next to me and held me tight, asking if everything was okay.

I looked at him, eyes flooded with tears. "Nothing, baby, everything is fine."

"Jasmine, what is going on? I know you are not crying for nothing. I told you you can talk to me about anything you feel the need to say."

"I fine, baby, trust me, it will be okay, I promise.

Now let's get to bed."

"But I…."

"Shhh, baby, I'm serious, it's nothing," I said as I placed my finger on his lips.

As months passed, no sign of my secret lover. I missed him. I would secretly send Johnathan love messages.

Dear Johnathan,

When you are away I count the days until you come back to me. I wish you never had to leave. I must say when we are apart, it feels like a hole in my heart. My life is not complete without you. It makes me feel oh so blue. I love you so much. And I love your touch. Hurry home to me. I miss you, you see!

In response I didn't receive anything. My husband began to get suspicious.

"Jasmine, can I ask you something?"

"Sure, what's up?"

"Would you care if we quit talking?"

"Marcus, why would you ask me that?"

"I'm just curious, that's all. I need to know how you feel so I know how to deal."

"Marcus…."

Before I could say anything, he butted in.

"Jasmine, I love you to the moon and back, till the end of the universe. I love you more than sand in the desert, as deep as the ocean blue, flower is less beautiful than you. I love you to the edge of the sky, either sunset or the sunshine."

"I love you too, but it's time that you know the truth."

"What are you talking about?"

"Marcus, the truth is that I'm having an affair."

"What?"

"Yeah, Marcus, I'm sorry."

"How could you? My wife of four years cheated on me. You know what, I'm not even mad for what you have done, I too have a confession. Remember me going on business trips? Well, I wasn't. I was going to see my other wife that I've been married to for three years."

That moment I began to feel weak. Suddenly I fell onto the floor, crying out. "How could you?" I said as I started smashing my face in my hands. "I hate you for what you've done, but I love you for what you've helped me become, a strong woman who will put her foot down. My mind keeps replaying how you played me like a stupid clown. You say I messed up, that I was wrong. I knew what was going on all along."

"Jasmine, get up, you not the only one hurt, you hurt me as well!" screaming at me.

"But Marcus, you knew what I've been through and for you to go out and get married on me. It seems like when you are here you don't make time for me. And for that I became lonely."

"Jasmine, I'm sorry but I can't do this anymore."

"But Marcus...."

"But Marcus nothing. I will have my lawyer mail you the divorce papers."

That night I lay in bed crying and he just didn't care. I sat and cried because I still did love him when he didn't deserve my love. Now I wished he would burn in hell.

"How could you do this to your wife, a woman who gave you everything? I see how much to you this marriage was worth, that you'd just throw me out in the dirt. For the next man I won't be able to open my heart. It doesn't matter how long we've been apart. The way that I loved you I will never love again."

I asked myself why did this have to end as I took a shot of wine before passing out. In my dreams, there were devils haunting my soul. Descending me slowly into hell was their goal. Lying, cheating, killing, deceiving, stealing. Taking over my every thought, wrecking all I found, all I'd sought. Driving me crazy, making me insane looking around, I was the only one to blame. As the devil began to call unto me, my heart started to pound. It was so silent, I heard nothing, it was so cold, my sweat froze, my lips froze and split, my skin was blue and burned. My thoughts, they were cursed. Through hell, with Satan by my side into paradise, a journey without hope.

From my sleep I began to cry upon "God." I felt like "God" didn't hear my cry. That moment I felt lost. Lost in a world that scared me to death. I began losing my breath. Lost as a woman. Lost in mind, lost in soul. As I began to cry out unto the "Lord" once more, Satan spoke.

"Where is your 'God' now?" Laughing.

Before I could answer, "God" appeared before me. "Here I am," he said in a mighty roar.

Satan became silent.

"My child, I heard your cry. I Will Never Leave You Nor Forsake You. Be strong and courageous," as he touched my forehead.

I was awakened. I sat up on the couch rocking back and forth, thinking about the experience I just had. I tried to call my husband but my calls were unanswered. So I decided to leave him a voice message.

Hey, Marcus,

I never meant to hurt you or to ever make you cry, there is nothing I want more in life than to have you by my side. We both have made mistakes. We need to put it in the past because the love I feel for you is one that I want to last. I have never loved another like I loved you from the start, you are very important to me. You are my love, my life, my heart! I love you, please come home.

I kissed the phone. Suddenly my phone started to ring. I got excited thinking it was Marcus returning my calls.

"Hey, baby, how are you feeling?"

"Who is this?" as I looked at the phone.

"You know who this is. Johnathan. Your lover."

I became silent.

"Hello? Hello? Jasmine, are you there?"

Taking my time answering, "Yeah, I'm here."

"What's wrong, talk to me."

"Everything is fine, Johnathan."

"Why haven't you been calling? I missed you."

"Johnathan, I needed some time and space to think about things."

"About us?"

"Yeah. And I told my husband that I've had an affair."

"Really? How did he take it?"

"Let's just say we are getting a divorce," I said, crying.

"I'm sorry, I didn't mean for it to happen like this."

"It's okay, Johnathan. He too had an affair. It hurts finding out he's been married to another woman."

"Damn. Wow. I'm speechless."

"So am I. Please come over and comfort me."

"Okay, give me a few minutes."

He arrived, greeting me at the door. Silence. Without cause he started kissing my neck. He knew just how to turn me on. Falling weak at the knees. Lifting me up, guiding me to the bedroom.

As I stared at him biting my lips, I screamed, "Fuck me! Your hard cock fits my pussy so nicely, fuck me hard, never go lightly."

As he began to stroke my pussy, I started cumming on his dick, very likely. My body started to tremble as I rode his cock. My pussy ached for this feeling around the clock. Grabbing my hips, "Slam me down on your dick so hard like a rock. I want to feel you cum inside and every fucking aftershock. Pull it out; watch it shine with wetness. Let me dive, fuck my mouth, you will soon confess…feelings of pleasure, lustily desires as I witness…your ass flexing, thighs shaking because I am your fucking goddess. Rise again, my body longs to have you inside of me. Pick a hole, slide it in, your cock is my security. Make me cum, I want to scream, fuck me hard, don't go easy. I'll be your doll, fulfilling your every fantasy. Forget the circumstances, give me your cock, I don't care how, I'll make your head spin as my pussy dances your dick, I will, wow, I know it's hot so just fuck me hard."

We made love for nearly three hours. That was the best sex I ever had as I cuddled under him.

"So what's up with your husband?"

"I told him the truth. I loved and respected him. I had no choice but to tell him. He didn't take it, besides he had an affair too so it really doesn't matter anymore.

All that matters is that we can be together. Right?"

"Have you heard the saying: two wrongs don't make a right? It is not acceptable to do a bad thing just because someone else has done it."

"Yeah, but he went out and got married to another woman."

"I understand that but you have to be a bigger person. I'm sorry that happened to you."

"It's okay, he is supposed to have his lawyer mail the divorce papers."

"I'm sorry I ruined your marriage."

"I've ruined my own marriage. In these moments, you start asking yourself questions you don't really want to know answers to: Would I rather touch myself than let him touch me? Is he seeing someone? You go long enough without, combined with the emotional vortex of shit you're living in, and you literally go a little bit crazy. I was emotionally beaten and physically broken at twenty-three years old," I said, rolling over, staring at the ceiling crying.

"It's okay."

"No, it's not. Sometimes he would leave without saying anything. I had my first God's-honest Will Hunting breakdown. I sobbed. Convulsed. Couldn't catch my breath. He could hear me through the floor vents in our upstairs bedroom. My pathetic loser husband...."

Before I could get another word out, he put his finger on my lips and said, "I will take care of you. Let me take care of your broken heart and show you how to fly, holding you gently by the hand and kissing your tears goodbye."

"At this moment I'm scared to love again."

"I understand, well, I'm about to go."

"Please don't take it personally. I do like you but it's just too soon. I hope you understand."

"I do and I want you in my life."

"So do I. Things take time. Call me when you get home!" I yelled, closing the door.

That night I thought about my husband. "Will you ever love me? When I'm missing you, I feel a million miles away. I long for your touch. I miss that angelic voice and the laughter that comes with it. I imagine your lips connecting with mine and your arms embracing me. I feel the distance that separates you from me. I can't imagine my life without you. No more separation. I sometimes dream of you and me happily ever after.

"But sometimes…

"My heart gets heavy not knowing for sure if you miss me. I often wonder if we'll ever be together or if you even care. I wonder if I just fill the void that fills the hole in your heart. The thought crosses my mind…will you ever love me like I love you?" I asked myself, holding his picture as tears raced down my face.

A couple days passed after I signed the divorce papers. Marcus returned not only by himself but with his wife.

"How could you bring her here?"

"Jasmine, I don't have time for you. I've come to get some of my things."

"Why are you doing this to me? We have been married nearly six years and you would destroy what we had?"

"Why does everything have to be about you? I wasn't happy and you weren't happy either. You're right, with all the attention and fake business trips I wanted to make our marriage work."

"Where did we go wrong? It used to be us. What happened to us? How did we get to this situation? How did it start? How did it end? I did you wrong, you did me wrong. I want you back, you don't want me back. I'm sad. Where do we go from here? What do I do with this feeling? The first moment not face to face reminds me how much you mean to me. I think it's time for me and you to go separate ways. I wish I could just push it all away. I know it's time for you and me to walk away. I'm sorry, Marcus," as I tried to hug him. "I've had enough. It's time for you to own up to your mistakes and realize that you messed up something good."

"I'm sorry but Marcus is my husband now."

I couldn't do anything but accept the fact that I'd

lost everything. The love of my life.

"Don't forget that we have a court day coming up," he said, walking out the door with his belongings.

March 12 was our court day. Divorce finalized. Leaving the divorce court, both Marcus and his wife were happy.

"I'm celebrating today! I've been waiting for this day for a long time! Finally, it's here!" Marcus said.

Wow. How could someone you love for so long be happy for a final divorce? The things that you work hard for doesn't mean anything. Down the drain.

That moment all I could do was feel bad. I went into a depressed mode. No phone calls. No contact. Isolation. I'm so lonesome I could cry. I started playing Hank Williams' song:

Hear that lonesome whippoorwill
He sounds too blue to fly.
The midnight train is whining low
I'm so lonesome I could cry.

Although the song captured a common feeling, I now know it is not just a feeling, but a condition that has a very real effect on the body, and as it turns out it is also a public health problem so much so that as the new year turned in Great Britain, the issues of loneliness and social isolation were added to a ministerial portfolio. A survey study there showed that hundreds of thousands of people had not spoken to a friend or relative in a month. That's a lot of silence in my life. Depression is real.

My depression was so bad that I had demons living inside of me. I stood in the kitchen with a gun to my head, crying in silence and fear, for the demons of darkness had driven me here. Cutting my heart right out of my chest, making me believe that the demons knew best. They were always there, sometimes just out of sight, waiting in the background till the time was right. These demons were destructive, knocking down the life I knew, hating everything about me; I hated myself, too. These demons couldn't be seen, but they were far from fairytales. They lived inside my mind; their evilness prevails.

With a gun pointed to my head, about to end the fight, I was too tired to continue. Giving up. Taking a sip of wine. *POW.* I pulled the trigger. My neighbor heard the noise. Falling onto the floor. My neighbor rushed in. Luckily she had a spare key.

"Oh my God, Jasmine, are you okay?"

I just lay there speechless, eyes rolling in the back of my head. I called 911.

Ring, ring, ring…

911: 911, what's your emergency?

Neighbor: Help…help…I need help.

911: Ma'am, can you please telling me what's going on?

Neighbor: My neighbor needs medical attention. She's laying on the floor motionless, barely breathing.

911: Okay, what's going on?

Neighbor: My neighbor just shot herself. I don't know why. I was in my apartment and all I heard was a gunshot, so I rushed over and saw her lying there on the floor. Please hurry and save her!

911: Okay, what's the address?

Neighbor: 923 Collway Drive.

911: Okay, I'm sending help, please stay on the phone with me until help arrives.

Neighbor: Okay.

"Jasmine, you're going to be okay," as he held me in my arms, rocking back and forth. That moment I fell into a coma. Was this the end of life? I hadn't had time to say goodbye to my family. I hadn't had time to make arrangements. No soul, no thought, no memory, no emotion from then on, everything in the world no longer had anything to do with me. I didn't care if any of them thought of me or commented on me. I wanted to lie here forever. Dead.

My deceased grandma came to me in my coma. It was not just a coma but also a vision.

"Grandmother!" I called out.

Then "God" appeared, pure as snow. Eyes sparkled like the stars above. Heaven was beautiful. His soft, smooth voice: "It's not your time, my child," touching my forehead as my eyes began to fill with tears. "Awaken."

"We got her to stabilize the guy in the ambulance."

"Where am I?"

"You are in good hands, you're going to be alright."

I spent nearly a week in the hospital due to the bullet wound. The doctors were surprised that I survived. The bullet was two inches away from my brain. Luckily they took a chance and removed it.

When I was released, I went to my cousin's home to spend the night. I felt the guilt of causing harm to myself over a man, that was not me. That was something I wouldn't do. I'm a strong black woman. The nightmare helped cure my mind. Also, by attending church, any church lost its appeal. The one thing that was missing from my life, sanctification through the Holy Ghost, was already in me according to the preacher. If what I had was enough to be a saint, it was not worth the trouble, I determined. It made no sense that I would spend the remainder of my days half empty spiritually. In church, I learned how good God is—that He can do anything. What was I supposed to do in return and how would I know it when I did it?

As I started to reflect on my life more, the more I reasoned about things, the more confusion stifled my thinking. But at the same time, I learned that I'm GOD'S MASTERPIECE.

"So God created man in His own image, in the

image and likeness of God He created him; male and female He created them" (Genesis 1:27).

Ask yourself: How do you see yourself? When you look in the mirror, what do you see? Do you think that you are less than others? Do you think that because you once failed that you are not valuable? God does not see you in this way. When God created you, He did not make a mistake! He made a perfect being. He made you represent Him the right way. He created you according to His Own Image and His likeness… reflecting His nature and character and representing Him in the world. When God designed you, He stamped His image in you. He made such a great effort to make something that is like Him. He sculpted you from nothing into something. You have been remarkably and wonderfully made.

Everything was coming together until I got that phone call from Johnathan. I'd done everything I could to ignore him, but temptation got the best of me.

Jasmine: Hello?

Johnathan: Hey, how are you feeling, did you miss me?

Jasmine: Yeah, I do.

Johnathan: How much?

Jasmine: Johnathan, I've changed. I'm trying to get right with "God." We can't continue to do this, I'm sorry.

Johnathan: But I love you, what, so you going to

give up on us even though you found out your husband cheated on you?

Jasmine: I'm sorr—

The phone hung up. Looking at the phone, I was confused, wondering why he would hang up the phone like that. I tried calling him back but his phone kept going to voicemail. Days passed by, no calls or sites from him. Maybe he got it. I was trying to change. I was relieved.

I attended church one Sunday. There he was, sitting in the back with a grin on his face. Wondering what the hell he was doing here, I said to myself. Fellowship came around, he walked up to me and shook my hand as if we didn't know each other.

"What the hell are you doing?" I whispered.

"I thought I'd come to church. We all need to hear the word once in a while, besides, you can't get rid of me," smiling as he walked off.

That whole time he was staring at me as if he wanted to kill me. The day the devil went to church. Very uncomfortable. The devil can't go to church; he can't be where Jesus is. The devil can't be where the Word is preached. The devil can't be where God is worshiped and praised.

Things turned from bad to worse. Johnathan would show up everywhere permitted, even have things delivered to my job, where my boss would question me. Tons of text messages and calls hammered my phone daily. Crying myself to sleep at night, wondering when this nightmare was going to end. Enough was enough. I finally gave in when the police didn't do anything. The devil lured me into a world of deception. Filling my heart with hate. You all alone, shivering and addicted to the wrath, as he vanishes in thin air like a thief in the night. During the times when you're supposed to be joyful and smiling bright for the whole world to see. He'll immediately zoom in to dampen your spirit and steal your joy, causing you to feel as low as any human being can be. When you're on bended knees, crying out to our heavenly father above and he's not answering as fast as you want him to. Satan will appear in a heartbeat, trying desperately to plead his case that no one's listening to you. You've doubted yourself constantly, because of the low-self-esteem concept he's embedded in your brain. He'll remind you time after time of the things you've lost, without mentioning once the things you're capable of gaining. Eventually you'll grow tired of his false prophecies and search endlessly for the answers to your questions. Eventually I dated Satan. I gave in. No one who could help. Not even "God."

Things started going from good to worse. Johnathan started abusing me.

"You promised me that you would protect me from

my family, from all the shit I went through. You promised to protect me from myself. You failed. I proved you wrong. You lied. All you did was protect your ego. You made me lose my mind. You moved us way too fast and I didn't get a chance to catch up. You just left me there in the rubble of myself. You sit there now and wonder where it all went wrong. You're when it all went wrong. You need to hurt the way I'm hurting. But I wouldn't wish that pain on my worst enemy. But I guess you're pretty close to Satan."

As time progressed I grew more and more scared of Johnathan. Sometimes I wished I still was with Marcus but that would never happen. He moved on and created another family. My heart was heavy. "Help. I am running out of time. I am losing my mind. I am so confused. I fell in love, now I am falling out of it. I am sorry, love. I think I am at the point of giving up. Oh, someone help me get out. I am ashamed of myself, but as for me giving up was the best solution. Please help me. I am losing my mind out of thin air. I promise I have learned my lesson. I feel like nobody is listening. Please hear my cry."

A stranger heard my cry, placing their hands on my shoulder, praying.

Heavenly Father,

I know that I have broken your laws and my sins have separated me from you. I am truly sorry, and now I want to turn away from my past sinful life toward you. Please forgive me, and help me avoid sinning again. I invite Jesus to become the Lord of my life, to rule and reign in my heart from this day forward. Please send your Holy Spirit to help me obey You, and to do Your will for the rest of my life. I know that I am a sinner in need of a Savior, my Lord and my God, have mercy upon my soul, a sinner. I believe that Jesus Christ is the Son of the Living God and that He died on the cross and shed His holy blood for the forgiveness of my sins. I believe Jesus rose again from the dead by the power of the Holy Spirit and sits on the right hand of God, and hears my prayer. Come into my heart, Lord Jesus, and wash all my sins away with Your holy blood. I invite you into my heart as my personal Savior, and will follow you the rest of my life. Your Word says you'll turn no one away, and that includes me. Therefore, I know you've heard me, and I know you've answered me, and I know I'm saved. Thank you, Jesus, for saving my soul. Father God, I confess that your son, Jesus Christ, is my Lord and Savior from this very moment. By faith in your word, I believe I am saved right now in Jesus' name. I pray all of this in the mighty name of my Lord God and Savior, Jesus Christ, Amen.

"Thank you," I said, looking up.

A sweet, soft tone spoke. "You're welcome, Jasmine."

"Wait. What? How do you know my name?"

"I am your guardian angel."

"My what?"

"Your guardian angel. Didn't you know! I have been assigned to you. Sent to care for your happiness throughout your life. To guide and protect you always, you are never alone. I am always by your side so call on me, I will come to your aid no matter what."

"If you, my guardian angel, tell me how…."

Before I could finish, they answered correctly.

"So, you are. Why is my life a living hell?"

"You made your life that way, Jasmine. It started with an altercation… something that triggered you more than you had realized. Some words that you let slide but made you feel like the traumatized child you refused to be. Some words that would change your life forever."

All I could say was "Wow. I really do have a guardian angel."

I just sat there in tears as my guardian read out my life story.

"You had a fucked-up childhood. This is a fact you had accepted and kind of acknowledged with an un-healthy survival mode that brought you to a mostly good marriage and no children. When I say fucked-up, I mean alcoholic father with suicidal thoughts. Verbal abuse. Cleaning blood off the walls and feces off the floor. Physical abuse by your father. A loving mother fighting her own demons, who then died from cancer in her fifties…. Nevertheless, trauma after trauma, you found the strength to push forward and move on, cutting people left and right from a life you needed to build alone to survive and remembering the words of your mother would always repeat: 'When you don't feel well, push through....' So that's what you was doing and how you dealt with your issues the best… until that day. Until you got triggered back to years of being verbally abused by your alcoholic father while your boundaries to isolate and work through it alone weren't respected. To anyone else, their mother-in-law screaming 'Shut up!' at them at the dinner table in front of their three kids while their husband doesn't move would have been a hard 'no.' To you…you were used to it from your childhood and you just needed to isolate and work through it to get by… but your wish to be left alone didn't get respected and there you were having to talk to a woman who was drunk on Scotch after repeating many times you just needed the evening to push through…. You talked to her…you weren't fine but you pushed through…."

I started questioning myself. Why did I? For her to feel better about what happened, to avoid being called difficult. For my husband not to be bothered. I disrespected myself so much that night and what I needed… I never talked to her for me… I knew talking to her was the worst thing I could do for me…. She was still drunk, and her words and her tone of voice are still haunting me while I type these words…. I didn't forgive

my husband for staying quiet, but I pushed through….
I was heartbroken and that evening opened my eyes to
what kind of man he was, the marriage I was in, the
compliance in which I lived, the person they thought I
was and the person I allowed them to see… the unwor-
thiness I attached to my own wellbeing…. But I pushed
through…then, one week later, the father I hadn't
talked to for twenty years died…. It shook me to the
core, but everyone around me kept saying I

shouldn't regret the person he was…that I shouldn't
be sad after what I had endured with him…that I had
no reason to grieve….

There was a knock on my door. I wondered who
could it be this time of night, pressing my ear to the door.

Jasmine: Hello?

Johnathan: Hello, Jasmine? (pausing)

Jasmine: What do you want, Johnathan?

Johnathan: I miss you. It seems like forever that
we last met.

Jasmine: Fuck you, Johnathan, you not worth my
time arguing with you.

Johnathan: Baby, please hear me out.

Ashley: Johnathan…

Johnathan: Please, Jasmine.

Ashley: You got five minutes or I'm calling the
police.

Johnathan: I love you, Jasmine. I really do and

don't know what I'd do without you…. I love you, baby, I swear it's true, don't ever leave me, 'cause I need you to love me too."

Before he could say another word, he found himself in my bedroom making love to me. I couldn't help it. I loved this man. Words couldn't begin to explain the feeling of him inside of me like a thief in the night. He slid right in the walls of my pussy when my hands gripped his ass. I felt his rhythm, he was smooth like a criminal, the type that knew just what he wanted precisely as he went in and out, out and in. My legs were open wide so he could move his dick freely to pleasure my insides. Mmmmmmmm, OMG! He felt so good, his dick had shifted gear.

"Fuck me! Fuck me! That's the spot, please don't stop, my dear, work that dick! Work that stick so I can wet."

His wood, OMG!

"I'm about to cum! Aaaaaaaaaaaaaaaaaaaaaaaaaaaaaaaaaaaaa! Baby…YOU FUCKED ME GOOD" (panting).

Three hours later we were done. Pulling back my hair, he began to tongue my ear. Mmmmmmm.

The Next Day

The next morning I woke up to breakfast in bed. He tried to be careful but burned all the bread trying to make sure that the coffee was hot. Charring a few pancakes, potatoes, and grits. The sausage I seared into smoldering bits. He made some muffins like miniature coals and roasted a package of cinnamon rolls. Breakfast and good dick. What a good combination.

As he sat next to me, staring me in my eyes, "Every moment I spent with you was like a beautiful dream come true. It was the best dream I ever saw, more colorful than a rainbow, your pretty voice is echoing in my ear, the splendid sound I ever hear. No nightingale's song can compare to your glamorous tone, those alighting brown eyes as bright as twinkling stars in the sky. I always wanted to hold your hand between my arms, close to my heart. My wish was to hug you hard and listen to the beat of your heart."

My eyes began to flood with tears. "I miss you too. My biggest fear in life was to be away from you. I've been living a nightmare since that came true day after day. Life is stuck in loneliness and misery. Why did fate have to take you away from me? I love you, Johnathan Banks. Omg. I can't believe I just said that. I'm sorry, that slipped out."

"You are good. That is why I took the liberty to ask you to marry me," getting on one knee.

"Wait. What? This can't be real."

"It's real," taking out a large diamond ring.

"Omg," as tears flowed.

"Jasmine, will you?"

"Yeah, Johnathan, I will love to be Mrs. Banks."

August 3 was our wedding day. Super excited.

"Welcome to New Beginnings. May this be a day of new beginnings the sun, like a fragrant apple; the summer air soft on the hands as the kiss of a child. May berries melt like honey on the tongue. May the heart rise in wonder at the clouds drifting across the sky. May the trails under boots be covered in pine quills, let the leaves rain down like memories in the autumn of the heart. May the snow beneath skis run as fast as watered silk, may the cold air kiss the cheeks, turn them red as summer's roses. May the rivers always flow with their unexpected beauty, the first freshets of snowmelt, the rush of early spring. May we always walk in gladness through whatever path or highway; may we always walk within the golden circle of love."

Looking into each other's eyes, "I promise to be yours forever if you promise to be mine forever."

We kissed.

A couple months later, I gave birth to a beautiful baby girl by the name of Añuli Ta'mia Banks. Everything was going well. Living the life I dreamed of. The life of Mrs. Banks. When you're living the dream, you let no one stop you from getting there. You try to make your life worth more than ever before because you now have another purpose for living. We're living the dream every day even though we may not know it because we are too busy trying to go a different way. When I live my dream, I live it to its full coverage because I know that mistakes happen and they happen for a reason. Don't try to be someone you're not, that just makes life even harder for you. I care for the ones who are true, not the ones who are through with their dreams. My dream really matters to me and no one's gonna take it away from me. I surround myself with people who are trying to get where I'm going and not trying to hold me down. So for all my people who are out there trying to live that wonderful dream, take a lighter and light in the sky and say, "I'm going to live the life of my dream."

Nine months later I got a surprise visit. My ex-husband, Marcus. At that time my husband was at work.

Knock, knock....

"Who is it?"

Silence.

Knock, knock....

"Who is it?"

My call was unanswered.

Opening the door, "Marcus," I said, shocked. "What are you doing here?"

"Can we please talk?"

"Talk? About what? There's nothing to talk about."

"Jasmine, I miss you."

"I don't miss...."

Before I could finish he placed me on the counter, proceeding to eat my pussy.

"Marcus. I'm married."

"Shhhhhh…," placing his finger on my lips. He proceeded eating my pussy. I knew it was wrong but it felt right.

"Marcus, fuck me slow and please don't stop. Pound into my body, God, it feels so good. I love the way you make me twitch. I'm gonna count to three and damnit, you better be in me. Fuck me hard, there ain't no better way, the harder you pound the faster I'll go, wanna see how many times you can make me scream? I wanna feel you, feel you right up in there...FUCK ME NOW!!! I'll just jump up on top...tell me you can resist me. I'll bet you a twenty says you can't...look here, see I'm right. Now fuck me."

In the middle of sex, my husband came home on his lunch break. As he proceeded down the hallway, he could hear me moan. As he reached our bedroom door, pressing his ear to the door, he heard, "MMMMMhmmmmm, Marcus, fuck me, oh, yes, fuck."

One black angry man busted through the door. "What the fuck, Jasmine? So I guess this is it, huh? After all the love bombing and fake feelings, you're finally ready to move on, you're ready to remember what it felt like when I didn't exist. You're excited to feel warmth in a new place. Because everything turned cold here. You made it this way, though. You turned off your feelings. Maybe you didn't even have any. Maybe I built a false persona of you in my head that was genuinely interested in me. I must be crazy to think all that time I spent investing in you, you were only pretending to like what I was saying. Like what I was giving to you. I didn't ask you for anything. I barely reached for a hand. But yet again I'll switch my feelings back to nothing and pretend like you never even stopped by. 'Cause it's that easy, right? I'm not that interested to remember. I'm not that hard to forget. You must have found someone better. So I'll pretend we ever met."

"Oh my God, baby, I'm sorry," as I jumped up from the bed. "I don't love him the way that I love you."

"Jasmine, you don't love me and don't feel compassion, don't you think that now I look my best? Though you look aside, you're thrilled with passion, putting your arms upon my chest. You are young, so sensitive and zealous, I am neither bad nor very good to you. Tell me, did you pet a lot of fellows?

You remember many arms and lips? You do? They are gone and haven't touched you any, gone like shadows, leaving you aflame. You have sat upon the laps of many, you are sitting now on mine, without shame. Though your eyes are closed, and you are rather thinking of someone you really trust after all, I do not love you either, I am lost in thought about my dear past. Don't you call this zeal predestination hasty, it is thoughtless and no good, like I set up this unplanned connection. I will smile when leaving you for good. You will go the pathway of your own just to have your days unwisely spent, don't approach the ones not fully grown, don't entice the ones that never burnt. When you walk with someone down the alley chatting merrily about love and all, maybe I'll be out, walking 'round shyly and again, by chance, I'll meet you, poor soul. Squaring shoulders, ravishing and winning, bending slightly forward, with an air kiss you will utter quietly, 'Good evening!' And I will reply, 'Good evening, miss.' Nothing will disturb my heart and spirit, nothing will perturb me, giving pain, he who's been in love will not retrieve it, he who's burnt will not be lit again. I think you and him should leave. I want a divorce and I'm taking our daughter."

"Baby. Please don't do this to me like this. I'm sorry, baby. If I can tell you how you make me feel, you bet it's all lies, but baby, it's all real."

"Jasmine, I don't want to hear more."

"Baby, please hear me out, listen to me, my life isn't what it used to be. You brought me happiness and love at times, I swear you're just an angel from way above. An innocent smile, laughter full of joy, your personality, oh boy, you're just perfect. My dream guy, with you I feel that I can do anything, even fly. I can face the whole world with you by my side. Today, I hurt you inside, I caused you pain, your first heartbreak. It was a regretful mistake. Please understand me, though, because deep inside me...down below I feel you deserve more than me getting you upset, you deserve to be adored, you deserve beyond the best because you not like the rest, you're more than I ever asked for. I love you for an eternity, that I swore, but can I love you so much that I would let you go? Forgive me for trying to, but I want you to know I can't help and feel bad that I caused you stress and infatuation so bad that I begin to feel that maybe it's best for our sep-aration because I messed up, I want you back because my life without you loses color, turns black. You were that light that guided me through this rocky road, you help me carry stress's heavy load. I'm who I am because of you and if you go I don't know what I'll do...to others this might be an exaggeration but baby, it's true, you're my life and motivation so you see that I'm sorry, babe. Yes, I'm pathetic for doing this, but I don't care what the world thinks of me. You're the one I care about, the one I love and need, please forgive me...let me cure your heart, let me put it back together, glue, tape, stitches, baby, I'll do whatever, even if it takes forever..." (sigh).

"Jasmine, I'm sorry, I can't. Leave."

"Okay. I will forever love you, Johnathan," as tears flowed down my face.

"Fuck," Johnathan said as he sat on the bed, holding his head.

After losing everything from the divorce, I wasn't ready to give up that easily. I was in love with Johnathan and Marcus. I was confused.

That night Marcus came home from work. I watched him sleep. Sleeping calm. Too calm for my liking. My evil eyes stared down and all else of you enticed my rageful desire. My mind was slowly bursting to bleed. My strong hands gripping to lust over him...and by the time I awakened that nightmare apparition was just watching you sleep. There was evil within, had crossed over, and all I wanted was to choke the life out of him. But my emotions were all twisted up just watching him sleep. I started fucking him.

"No, Jasmine, what are you doing?"

Placing my finger on his lips, I began to grind on his dick hard as I stared in his eyes. He couldn't resist.

"Fuck me," I said repeatedly. "Fuck me, Marcus. Make me scream. I want to scream your name, make me hot and wet for you, I want to play a game. Tell me what turns you on so that I can be your fantasy. Everything I do will be for you. I want to know how you feel with your dick inside of me when I suck on it in my mouth, and when you stick it in my pussy and in my ass. I want to know, I want to know everything about you, and everything you feel. I want to do everything to you that makes you get hard, I want to watch you as I turn you on. I want to see your dick harden because of me, I want to see you begin to perspire and watch your balls change as I turn you on. I want to make you breathe heavily, I want to kiss every part of your manhood, I want to make you moan, I want you to shove your penis down my throat, as far as it will go. Then I want you to fuck me, Marcus. Make me scream your name. Fuck me hard, then fuck me soft. Over and over again. Pull my hair while you fuck me, caress my breasts with your hand. Pound and pound my pussy, slap my ass until it's nice and red. Place me on my knees, make me so horny I beg, make me beg you to suck it, then move around my head. I want to hurt tomorrow so fuck me good tonight. Let me be your fantasy. Get it while it's tight. Fuck me harder, Marcus. Oh, please don't make me plead, I want for you to pound me your dick is all I need, fuck me harder, Marcus. I want to make you cum, fuck me till I scream your name, fuck me till I'm numb, fuck me harder, Marcus. Put it in my ass and spank me while you hit it. Hit that ass with class, spank me as I'm screaming, screaming out your name, spank me till I'm crying and then spank me again, spray my mouth with deep throat, then shove it down me as I lay.

"Make me gasp for air as your dick goes all the way. Fuck me inside my mouth. Push it in and out, watch me as I suck it. The whole thing without a doubt, fuck me upside down, fuck me standing up. Fuck me in a doorway while your dick is in my butt. Don't forget that pussy, pound it till it's dry. Shove your dick inside me until you reach my eye. Use your sex toys on me, go down on me. Turn on my vibrator, move it all around. We can both enjoy the pleasure. Fuck me harder. Pleasure me, then hurt me. Treat me like a sex doll. Fuck me like you would if the body had no limits and do me like you should."

Thirty minutes later he nutted. Licking the nut from his dick, I lay in his arms. The next day I woke up to him smiling.

"Good morning, Jasmine."

"Oh my God, what the hell am I doing here? Ashamed. I can't believe we fucked."

"Jasmine, it's okay, I wanted it."

I had to go. At home. Ashamed. Questioning myself about what I just did. I felt dirty. How could this be? Asking "God" for forgiveness.

"Lord, I kneel before You in humble submission and pray that in Your mercy and kindness You would help me to simply let go of all the fears and worries, problems and doubts, guilt and disappointments that seem to be filling my heart and mind so often, during the course of a day.

"Maybe it's best that I set myself free. Is it possible that I liked you more than the person I am? Or maybe it's only the sadness of a lover," I said to myself.

As I sat in despair I could hear my coworker say, "Beware. They may have game…but their tongues speak with lies. Pleading to kind hearts for a prize."

I was head over heels with both of these guys. I was in too deep. I've got nothing left. I have no life. I'm dead inside. I'm sorry. I'm finished. I've sold my soul to both. Crying. Holding a gun to my head. Wanting to end it all. As tears flooded my eyes, I pulled the trigger. This time I didn't make it. I tried to overcome the damage I've caused, but it got the best of me. So now. No more worries. I'm free….

www.ingramcontent.com/pod-product-compliance
Lightning Source LLC
Chambersburg PA
CBHW060220170726
48004CB00014B/820